Flood!

NATURE'S DISASTERS

Flood!

John Waters

A LUCAS · EVANS BOOK

CRESTWOOD HOUSE
New York
Collier Macmillan Canada
Toronto
Maxwell Macmillan International Publishing Group
New York   Oxford   Singapore   Sydney

Austin

10-91

10.95

a42543

Dedicated to Hap and Coleen

COVER: Closed for business. This general store in West Alton, Missouri, was one of the casualties of the 1986 Mississippi flood.

FRONTIS: A tidal wave struck the Japanese coast in May 1983. One hundred and four people drowned.

PAGE 7: A storm surge crashed ashore a barrier beach on Cape Cod, Massachusetts, during the 1978 blizzard. Towns were flooded and houses were torn to bits.

PHOTO CREDITS: *Cover*, Official U.S. Coast Guard Photo; *Frontis*, Takaaki Uda, Public Works Research Institute, Japan/National Geophysical Data Center; *Page 7*, Richard Kelsey, courtesy Kelsey-Kennard, Chatham, MA; *Pages 8–9*, Official U.S. Coast Guard Photo; *Page 10*, Massachusetts Coastal Zone Management; *Page 15*, American Red Cross Photo; *Page 16*, American Red Cross Photo; *Page 17*, American Red Cross Photo; *Page 19*, Official U.S. Coast Guard Photo; *Page 20*, Ralph R. Shroba/USGS; *Page 21*, Wallace R. Hansen/USGS; *Page 22*, Wallace R. Hansen/USGS; *Page 24*, Jill Kastner; *Pages 32–33*, Alison Forbes/N. E. Stock Photo; *Page 35*, Massachusetts Coastal Zone Management; *Page 37*, Takaaki Uda, Public Works Research Institute, Japan/National Geophysical Data Center; *Page 40*, Air Weather Service/Public Affairs; *Page 42*, American Red Cross Photo.

BOOK DESIGN: Barbara DuPree Knowles   DIAGRAMS: Andrew Edwards

LIBRARY OF CONGRESS CATALOGING-IN-PUBLICATION DATA

Waters, John.
   Flood! / by John Waters.—1st ed.
     p.   cm. — (Nature's disasters)
   SUMMARY: Examines the nature, origins, and dangers of floods and discusses the different kinds and their damaging effects.
   ISBN 0-89686-596-7
   1. Floods—Juvenile literature.   [1. Floods.]   I. Title.   II. Series.
GB1399.W39 1991   551.48'9—dc20   90-45371

Crestwood House
Macmillan Publishing Company
866 Third Avenue
New York, NY 10022

Collier Macmillan Canada, Inc.
1200 Eglinton Avenue East
Suite 200
Don Mills, Ontario M3C 3N1

First Edition

Printed in the United States of America   10 9 8 7 6 5 4 3 2 1

Contents

Flood!

Everyone is familiar with the story in the Bible of Noah and the ark. It tells how God was upset with the people of the world and decided to send a flood to wash away all that was bad. God told Noah that there would be so much water it would cover the entire earth.

However, God wanted to save all the different kinds of animals. He told Noah to build a giant ark. Noah was given exact instructions on how to build the ark. Noah's wife and sons helped him finish the task. When the huge craft was built, Noah took aboard a male and female of every living creature.

After that it rained for 40 days and 40 nights. Even the highest mountains were covered by water. When the rain stopped, Noah sent out a dove. The dove flew back to the ark twice. The third time it did not return, so Noah knew that the waters had receded enough for the dove to find a place to land. God spoke to Noah again. He said that Noah could tell his children that never again would a flood be

St. Louis during the flood of 1986. The Missouri River rose so high it changed its course!

Tons of rock cover what is left of an automobile that was buried by ocean waves during the great blizzard of 1978 in New England.

sent to earth to destroy mankind. Then a rainbow appeared. God said that whenever Noah saw a rainbow, he should remember what God had said.

WHAT IS
A FLOOD?

All life on our planet depends on water to live. We drink it from our taps and wells. In our freshwater ponds, streams and lakes, we swim in it, fish in it, boat in it. Saltwater oceans cover three-fourths of our earth's surface. Sixty-five percent of the human body is composed of water. But when a **flood** occurs, water can be a deadly killer.

A flood is the covering or submerging with water of an area that is normally dry. Floods are created in many different ways. Torrential rainstorms can hit low-lying areas where the water cannot run off quickly enough. **Earthquakes,** disrupting the earth's crust, can unleash whole lakes that come flowing down into valleys. Man-made **dams** can break, causing floods. When undersea volcanoes erupt, they can create giant waves and send them across the ocean to flood coastal towns and villages hundreds of miles away. But more often floods are created as a result of **tropical storms** or **hurricanes.**

FLOODS CREATED BY TROPICAL STORMS

Hurricane Camille

It was just such a tropical storm that unleashed floods in Virginia in the summer of 1969. Hurricane Camille had already spent its rage and fury along the Gulf of Mexico by August 18. As the tail end of the storm neared Virginia from the south, it was all but dead. To the north was a cold front with massive thunderstorms. It too was heading toward Virginia.

Hurricane Camille's winds picked up warm, moist air from the Atlantic Ocean and clashed with the approaching cold front. They met over the Tye and Rockfish river valleys. The result was solid sheets of rainfall.

The hard rain produced more than 31 inches in six hours in some spots. The Rockfish River rose almost 30 feet. The rivers and creeks of the valleys could not contain the onslaught, so the waters tore over the banks and swamped the lowlands. All this occurred at night when most people were in their beds.

The water cascaded into the valleys. A sizable chunk of mountain, weakened by the storm, began to move. It slid down into the valleys, carrying with it boulders, mud and giant trees by the thousands. By the time the **landslide** was over, some farms were buried under 30 feet of soil, trees and rocks. More than 125 people died in the flood and hundreds were left homeless.

Camille is an example of one of the more common causes of floods—the heavy rains that accompany tropical storms. Rainstorms that form over the warm waters of the **tropics** are loaded with moisture. When conditions are right, these giant storms head toward land, bringing promise of many inches of rain. This causes streams and rivers to overflow, producing inland floods. Many of these tropical storms are either born or intensify over the warm waters of the Gulf of Mexico.

Hurricane Fifi

In 1974 a storm that swept through the Caribbean Sea south of the Gulf of Mexico caused massive floods when it struck the country of Honduras. Weather forecasters throughout the Gulf of Mexico and Central America were following the track of the storm. They alerted every country in its path. The government of Honduras was warned 48 hours in advance. However, being a poor country, its outlying districts had poor communications. That meant thousands of people had no idea that a killer storm was bearing down upon them.

At first the rains came. Then the winds blew in, reaching

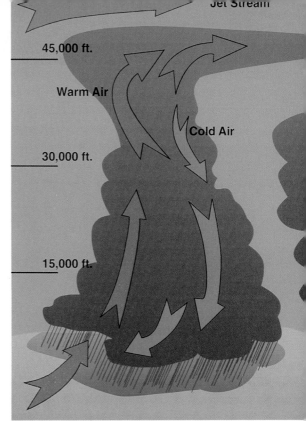

Jet Stream

45,000 ft.

Warm Air

Cold Air

30,000 ft.

How a severe thunder-storm develops. Masses of warm, humid air rise upward and form a cloud. At about 50,000 feet the cloud stops rising and forms a cap. Winds blow the cloud cap horizontally. Rain then begins to fall.

15,000 ft.

speeds of 140 miles an hour. While the winds raged, the rains came in torrents. In a day and a half, two feet of rain fell! If a city such as Atlanta, Georgia, receives an inch of rain, some 2.36 billion gallons of water fall to the ground. If two feet of rain were to fall in one storm over the city, almost 57 billion gallons of water would drop down. This much rain fell in various places all over Honduras.

Hundreds of people were left homeless from the floods and more than 8,000 died. After the storm, rescue workers in airplanes surveyed the damage. They saw people mirac-ulously alive, hanging on to anything that was above the rapidly flowing floodwaters. Helicopters were called in, and rescuers plucked survivors from roofs, trees, poles and the tops of hills.

For the survivors, what came after the rescue was worse. Their crops and livestock had been washed away. Bananas and coffee plants, important export crops, were wiped out. Corn, rice, beans and other vital food crops were all destroyed. They had no food, no homes, no farms. They suffered total devastation. It would be years before Honduras recovered from the floods of Hurricane Fifi.

SEASONAL FLOODING

The Great Spring Floods

In May 1990 heavy rainstorms began over the Gulf of Mexico and headed north into the southwest corner of the United States. The storms not only had a lot of rainfall, but they also stayed around for a long time. In Texas waters from rain-swollen Lake Livingston poured into the Trinity River. The flow was so great it flooded more than 200 square miles along the river.

The Lake Livingston Dam had been built to control floods. In fact, many such dams are built all around the world. The idea of the dams is to hold back floodwaters and allow an even flow of water so riverbanks do not overflow. However, there was so much water the engineers controlling the dam had no choice. They had to release tons of water even though this would flood homes in the area below the dam and along the river. This area covered some 990 square miles; over 20 percent was flooded.

More than a dozen **floodgates** had to be opened. The result was a record 100,800 cubic feet of water per second passing through the Lake Livingston Dam. This flow broke a record that had been set almost 50 years earlier.

Floods destroyed crops as far east as Arkansas and Louisiana. More than 700,000 acres of farmland in Louisiana were covered with water. In Hot Springs, Arkansas, more than 13 inches of rain fell, knocking out the hot springs that give the town its name. The town was hit with a **flash flood.** The electric pumps that bring up 140-degree water for the bathhouses were damaged. It took a week to get the pumps working again.

When floods hit the town of Elba, Alabama, in 1990 not only houses were damaged. Cemeteries were flooded as well, and coffins from shallow graves bobbed to the surface.

Elba, Alabama, 1990. The only means of transportation at this cross-road is by boat.

What made these floods so unusual was that they set all-time records in so many states. For example, at Little Wichita River in Texas, 6 million gallons of water roared past a monitoring station each minute. This was almost twice the amount of water of the flood record set in 1966. In Oklahoma the amount of flow at the Red River Dennison Dam broke the record set in 1935. And the record flow on the Red River in Arkansas broke the old mark set in 1938.

According to some scientists, the record-setting Texas floods of 1990 were caused by **global warming,** or the "greenhouse effect." This is the **theory** that changes in the earth's atmosphere will make the gases in it act like the glass roof and walls of a greenhouse: The atmosphere traps more heat near the earth. This would cause the earth to heat up too much. Such global warming may have heated the water and caused faster evaporation in the Gulf of Mexico. With more water vapor in the lower portion of the atmosphere, little storms grew into big ones laden with heavy moisture. These storms transformed tiny streams into raging rivers.

The entire first floor of this house is completely underwater.

If the theory of global warming is true, in about 60 years sea levels will rise three to five feet. Coastal areas in places like New England and Louisiana will be partially underwater or subject to flooding for many years. Much planning is needed in case this takes place. Sewage treatment plants, nuclear reactors, hospitals and schools cannot be built in areas likely to be flooded.

The Salt Lake Flood

Record rains fell in Utah during September 1982. They were followed in the winter by the heaviest snows to hit the Wasatch Mountains in a century. In May there was an unexpected heat wave and melting snows roared down the slopes. The water raced along the **flood plain,** but it also gushed over into Salt Lake City. Although the water finally left the city, much of it remained in the plains and in Great Salt Lake throughout the summer.

The next winter brought another deep snowfall in the Wasatch Mountains. **Meteorologists** checked the depth of it and could not believe what they found. The snow the winter before had been the heaviest in a hundred years. But now this one matched the previous year's.

All during the winter people filled more than a million sandbags. The sandbags were placed on the riverbanks to keep them from overflowing when the snows would melt in the spring. On the last day of May a heavy thunderstorm struck, and a whole new series of floods began.

Great Salt Lake (about the size of the state of Delaware) was growing larger. Water burst through a **dike** and flooded the evaporating ponds of the Great Salt Lake Minerals and Chemicals Corp. Some 30 square miles of salt ponds that

When the Missouri and Mississippi rivers overflowed in 1986, nearby homes were hard hit. And even horses suffered. In one stable 55 horses were stranded shoulder deep in water for two days.

produce 200,000 tons of sulfate potash a year were now underwater.

As the lake grew larger it covered valuable **wetlands.** Marshes, home to many species of wildlife, were covered with salt water. Roads were submerged. Dikes were many feet underwater. An amusement park built on the shores of the lake became an island. During the height of the flood, the park's owner was able to paddle a boat across the dance floor. Fortunately, there was little loss of human life or livestock because people had been warned beforehand. Also, the flood had built steadily, allowing plenty of time for people to protect themselves.

FLASH FLOODS

Some of the most dangerous floods are flash floods. They result from tropical storms, dam failures or from combinations of rain and melting snow. Flash floods flow much faster than the Great Salt Lake flood.

Big Thompson River

The Big Thompson River flows from the Rocky Mountains through the Big Thompson Canyon on its way to the South Platte River. It is a journey of 78 miles. It is such a tiny river that anyone looking at it would not consider it much of a flood threat. However, for a few hours during July 31,

A house is left on a precarious perch after the Big Thompson River flash flood.

This pickup is nearly buried in the blanket of sand deposited by the floodwaters of the Big Thompson River.

1976, it was indeed a big river and a destructive one as well. It played a major role in a flash flood that literally tore the canyon and its people to pieces.

All through the canyon, motels and campgrounds were filled with vacationers. People waded in the refreshing waters, went for swims, hiked or tried to catch fish. Late in the afternoon, thunderstorms formed and headed for the canyon. It had rained many times before and no one seemed concerned about the latest series of storms. Even the weather forecast stations in the area only warned that there could be some local flooding.

Then strange things happened. **Thunderheads** began to break down and the whole line of storms began to weaken. Remaining were 12 miles of intense storms that hovered over the upper third of the Big Thompson Canyon.

A washed-out dam along the Big Thompson River after the flash flood of 1976.

At first it sprinkled and then it began to pour. By 6:30 P.M. there were cloudbursts everywhere. Rain crashed down from the sky for almost five hours. It rained so hard that a state trooper said the pockets in his raincoat filled with water in an instant. Another state trooper described the raindrops as being half an inch wide and dropping straight down.

At 8 o'clock, word came into the Colorado Highway Patrol that U.S. Highway 34 had washed out in the canyon. A trooper was sent to investigate. When he got to the canyon, he realized how dangerous the situation was. He radioed that everyone had to get out as fast as they could. Then he realized his own patrol car was being washed away. He said that the mountainside was falling on top of him and that he was afraid he would drown. Inside of a few minutes, he had to abandon his patrol car and swim to higher ground.

A foot of rain had fallen in the narrow part of the canyon in less than five hours. That meant that in some areas the Big Thompson River had risen by more than 20 feet!

The water cascaded down the banks of the canyon, tearing away at everything in its path. Campers living in tents or trailers were swept away, as were their trucks and cars. Buildings were ripped apart. A motel register was discovered the next day, with 23 names listed. No guests were found, however, as the motel had disappeared.

Italy's Famous Flood

In the fall of 1966, wild rainstorms and high winds ravaged all of Europe. They were violent over parts of Italy. What would have been an average rainfall for that area in a period of six months cascaded down in a period of two days.

The Arno River in Florence, Italy, after the great flood of 1966. The water rose 15 feet above street level.

There was also an accumulation of snow in the mountains. When the storms came with warm winds they created two disastrous forces—heavy rains and melting snow. The rivers swelled and created **avalanches** of trees, mud and boulders.

Muddy waters ran through the streets of some of the towns located along the banks of the rivers. The mud and water was so deep that cars and buses were swallowed up. All communication was cut off, making it impossible for people to move around unless they had boats.

One of the hardest-hit cities was Florence. Damage done there was felt around the world. Florence houses 40 museums with some of the greatest art treasures of the world. There are also glorious palaces and cathedrals and some of the world's most famous historic buildings.

Normally, the famous Arno River flows through the city at a gentle 4 miles an hour. Once the surge of floodwaters hit, the river overflowed its banks. The water did not merely seep over. It rushed over, tearing along at a speed of 40 miles an hour.

The river spilled into the city until the water reached a height of 15 feet. The water covered two stories of the buildings, lingering in the city for 24 hours before it slowly began to recede. During the flood, the people of Florence could barely save themselves, let alone any of the priceless art objects.

Once the people were safe and able to find shelter and food, the task of saving the art began. Experts and workers from all over the world poured into Florence to help. Millions of books and the paintings of the masters were restored. The famous buildings and the artwork inside were cleaned and restored. Amazingly, one year after the flood, Florence was back to normal. The galleries, libraries and museums were open again. Still, if the Arno River were to overflow its banks again due to a massive storm, chances are Florence would be flooded once more.

EARTHEN DAMS AND LEVEES

People who live in valleys or on the flood plains beneath or next to **earthen dams** or **levees** risk being subject to sudden flooding. Earthen dams are built across rivers to dam them up. Levees are built alongside rivers to keep them from overflowing. Earthen dams and levees can fail because of earthquakes, **erosion** from within, poor engineering and construction, and avalanches from surrounding mountains. However, the most common cause of failure is excessive rainfall.

When it rains a great deal, the water behind the dam or levee builds up and finally flows over the top. This action washes away the upper part of the levee or dam and carves out deep ruts. Eventually the dam or levee is so weakened that the pressure of the water behind it soon destroys the structure, releasing tons of water all at once.

An earthen dam.

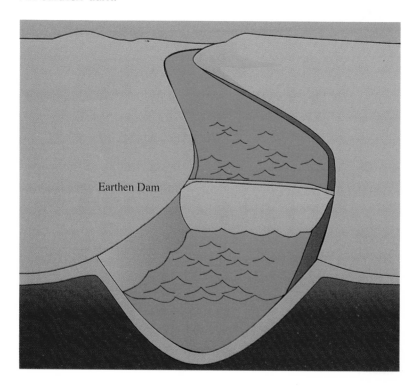

Earthen Dam

The Johnstown Flood

Up above the city of Johnstown, Pennsylvania, some 15 miles away, was the man-made earthen South Fork Dam. Behind the dam was a **reservoir** some 2 miles long, almost 1 mile wide and 70 feet deep. On an average day it held almost 20 million gallons of water. The dam holding it back from the valley below was made of earth. It was 72 feet high, over 900 feet long and 270 feet wide at its base. People living in the valley sometimes wondered what would happen if the dam ever gave way. On May 31, 1889, the people of Johnstown found out.

The day before, it had begun to rain. The rainfall was heavy and continued all night. By the next morning, the river feeding the reservoir behind the dam had begun to rise at the rate of one foot an hour. As water began washing over the top of the South Fork Dam, crews were sent to unclog drainage culverts and spillways. These are built below the top level of the dam so excess water can spill through them and not over the top of the dam. Because the spillways were neglected, they were clogged and the men sent to clean them were too late. At noon on May 31, the water began eating away the earth. At a few minutes to three, the center of the dam broke and the structure collapsed. A wall of water 40 feet high surged down into the valley.

The rampaging water raced through the village of South Fork. It was spared because it was set on high ground. But the village of Mineral Point, located on lower ground, was wiped out. On the way to Johnstown the water crashed into a railroad yard and smashed into locomotives, freight cars and passenger cars. Some were flung aside, while others

An earthen levee.

were swept along in the debris pile. Farther on, the wall of water gobbled up a passenger train and everyone aboard. Nothing stopped the rushing water. It even moved on to a large plant that manufactured wire. There it picked up wire and steel coils. It approached a barn full of hay and horses and wiped it out.

Then the wall struck Johnstown. Accounts from survivors say they heard a terrible roar and saw a dense, black cloud. Later the black cloud was called a death mist and was thought to be the remains of the fires from the wireworks.

Ten minutes after the water hit, the city of Johnstown was destroyed. The wave split three ways. The main wave carved away the center of the city, slamming into a bridge. The bridge held the clogged debris and formed a debris dam. The blockage created a lake behind the bridge, and about 600 people, barely alive, tried to climb out. Then terrible luck foiled their attempts. Oil from a leaking railroad car caught fire and the tons of debris started burning. Most of the people escaped, but some 100 were trapped alive and their death screams were heard above the sound of the churning water.

By the next day, breaks occurred in the debris dam at the bridge. Soon the waters drained away. The devastation was complete. The middle of the city was gone. The residential section was also gone, except for a few homes built on the sides of hills. Only a few stone buildings were left standing.

CONCRETE DAMS

Dams made of concrete are considered to be stronger and more stable than those made of earth. Such dams are often used to create hydroelectric power. They are usually constructed to seal off a deep river valley. Water builds up behind the dams, creating reservoirs, or artificial lakes. The deep water improves fishing and boating in the area. The real purpose, however, is to have the water turn giant **turbines** to produce inexpensive electrical power.

Some **concrete dams** are used to control floods as well as to produce energy. These dams are built across rivers that have a history of flooding. The dams hold back floodwaters in a man-made lake. The water is released through floodgates at a gradual pace so it does not overflow the banks of the rivers below the dams. Ideally there will never

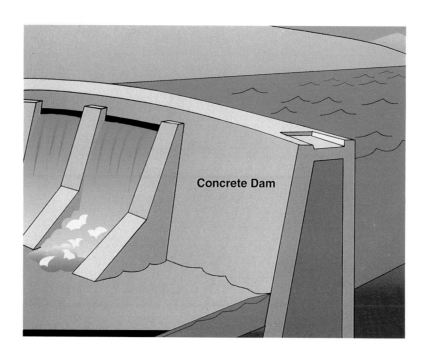

A concrete dam.

be so much water that the lakes behind the dams will overflow. However, sometimes that is exactly what occurs.

The Vaiont Dam

The Vaiont Dam was built in the Italian Alps in the north-eastern corner of Italy. It was a massive structure of concrete some 873 feet above the river valley below. Along the river valley were many small villages, including the village of Langarone with almost 2,000 inhabitants.

There was much rain in the fall of 1963. The extra water loosened earth and rocks on the slopes of the mountains surrounding the reservoir. Mount Toc, 6,000 feet tall, was especially shaky. On the night of October 9 of that year, part of Mount Toc fell into the reservoir.

Within minutes an avalanche of earth, mud, rocks and trees followed, crashing into the lake. This caused tons of water to spill out over the top of the dam and into the valley below.

The next day revealed a gruesome scene. Hardly a building was left standing in the village of Langarone. Rescuers found nothing but piles of stones. In the other little villages below the dam, most of the population had perished.

What set this flood disaster apart was what happened afterward. A court of inquiry was set up to learn if the disaster could have been prevented. There were many questions to be answered. Had the dam been poorly designed? Had it been built in a bad location? Had authorities warned people properly?

Eventually it was decided that the site of the dam was very poor. If a proper study had been done before it was built, the dam never would have been situated where it was because of the frequency of earth movements. The courts learned that even before the dam had been built, there were concerns about the safety of Mount Toc. And even as the dam was being built, workers and engineers were fearful of a disaster at the site.

Once the inquiry was over, the Vaiont Dam was shut down. The villages that were leveled were built up again.

The Aswan High Dam—A Good Idea?

There are records that date back as far as 3100 B.C. of the Nile River in Egypt flooding each year. What caused the annual flooding were the heavy summer rains that fell on

Egypt's Aswan High Dam.

neighboring Ethiopia. During all those years, the people of Egypt tried to control the flooding with levees, canals or dams called barrages. These were piles of earth, stones and even concrete. All that control was necessary because the water volume often rose 3,500 times from its lowest point.

In modern times the Aswan High Dam was built to stop the flooding and to produce electrical power. It was finished in 1971. The dam, more than 2 miles wide, is 365 feet high. Engineers calculate that it contains enough stone to build 17 Great Pyramids. The dam created 300-mile-long Lake Nasser.

Since the dam makes water available year-round, there are no more droughts. And millions of acres of new farmland have been opened. However, farmers have a new problem. Trapped behind the dam is the rich and fertile silt once carried by the Nile and spread across the countryside during the summer floods. Each year these nutrients renewed the land. Now farmers have to bring in artificial fertilizers. Also, salts accumulate in the soil beyond the dam. The annual floods used to carry the salts away. Almost 20 years later, engineers are still trying to resolve the many problems created by the Aswan High Dam.

COASTAL FLOODING

Oceans cover about 71 percent of the surface of the earth. When winds and other natural events cause the ocean water to act up, flooding along the shores results. Ocean storms with strong winds pile water up on a coast, raising the level of the sea in that area. These **storm surges** cause **coastal flooding.**

Ocean flooding in 1978 made a shambles of cottages along the New England coast.

Coastal flooding most often occurs as a result of severe storms, either tropical in nature, such as hurricanes or cyclones, or winter storms. In the Pacific, these storms blow onto the shores of the western United States, sometimes pushing huge waves onto the beaches. Along the eastern shores, storms travel from the west or ride up from the south. When they reach the open ocean, they intensify. The push of the storms makes a higher water level. Their raging winds build huge waves that crash on unprotected beaches and dunes.

In the winter of 1978 the northeastern coast of the United States experienced severe flooding. It was the result of a combination of high winds, high tides and a storm surge.

The high winds came at a time of unusually high tides. In areas south of the city of Boston, Massachusetts, waves crashed ashore, leaping over the seawall that had been built to protect houses and cottages. The waves either broke through the seawall or smashed over the top. The wild action of the waves tore the houses into bits. Low-lying towns were flooded with ocean water and ice, making it impossible for people to escape from their homes.

In January 1987, during another storm in the same area, a part of the outer **barrier beach** off Cape Cod broke away. The beach, eight miles in length, protected the mainland. When the waves broke through a part of it, the water began to spill into a quiet bay. After a few months, the hole in the beach became wider and wider. That meant that more water came into the bay and that a whole stretch of the mainland was exposed. Water eroded the shore and flooded it with each high tide, especially during storms. Some houses crashed into the sea. Others that were doomed to the same fate were torn down and carted away to the dump. Home owners hated to see their homes demolished, but they had no choice. Each winter the land the houses were built on was washing away and simply disappearing. The flood damage caused by the storm of 1987 is still taking place.

Tsunamis

Another kind of coastal flooding is caused by long, low sea waves. These waves can be caused by volcanoes, landslides, earthquakes or explosions. Often these waves are called tidal waves, but the tides really have nothing to do with them. They are correctly called **tsunamis,** which is a Japanese word describing long, low waves.

A tsunami in early (ABOVE) and later (BELOW) stages of withdrawal from the Japanese coast in 1983. This tidal wave caused about $800 million in property damage.

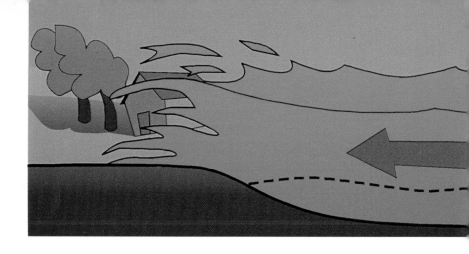

Tsunamis are very hard to detect on the open sea. Thus it is important that **seismologists,** scientists who study earthquakes, keep track of ocean tremors and warn of possible tsunamis. These waves are dangerous because of the tremendous speeds at which they move. The deeper the water, the faster the waves travel. In water several miles deep, the tsunamis can travel upward of 600 miles an hour! When the waves near shore and shallow water, they slow down. Then they begin to build in height. When the tsunamis hit shore they may be 50 to 100 feet tall!

Tsunamis travel thousands of miles without weakening. They usually strike islands or coral reefs in their way and then continue on. If they strike a huge land mass, such as a continent, they either die or they bounce back and go in the opposite direction.

WARNING SYSTEMS

Weather Satellites

What a boon it was to weather forecasting when satellites were sent aloft to help in predicting weather. From the beginning, the satellites were invaluable in flash-flood fore-

ing animals, trucks, cars and equipment, to high ground.

If warnings are given days or weeks in advance, then farmers try to harvest crops. The Red Cross and other disaster-relief agencies can then be fully prepared to handle people flooded out of their homes. Such help is vital because a lifetime of work can disappear. Family homes can be destroyed along with personal belongings. Appliances such as television sets and refrigerators can be replaced. But personal papers, family photograph albums and items handed down from generation to generation can be gone forever. Other than losing loved ones, these lost treasures often cause the most grief to the flood survivors.

FLOOD PREVENTION AND CONTROL

There are many systems in place today to help prevent or control floods. Throughout history people have constructed flood-control dams across rivers and dikes and levees alongside rivers to keep then from overflowing during high-water times. Canals are used to drain off excess water in emergencies. Sometimes streams and rivers are diverted to avoid populated areas.

Entire lowland areas are also under constant study. Through the years people have been allowed to fill in wetlands to build their roads, houses, shopping centers, schools or entire business areas. Today some 200,000 to 400,000 acres of wetlands are lost in the United States every year. The numerous bottomlands, bogs, marshes and swamps are valuable in flood prevention and control. They act as giant sponges that soak up large amounts of water and slowly let the water run off. When lowlands and wetlands are filled in, floods cannot be prevented and more are likely to occur.

Guests at this Alabama motel had barely enough time to check out before floodwaters hit in 1990.

Authorities constantly warn people not to build where there might be flooding. Despite warnings, people live either right on the coast or next to rivers and streams. Some live in the middle of wetlands. Many come face-to-face with storms or floods all of their lives. Outsiders ask why they live where they do. The residents say they enjoy life because of the magnificent views. They also like the closeness and the challenge of nature. A few of these people even believe that they can control nature.

Flood Safety Rules

The spread of disease is a danger during and immediately following a flood. Waste disposal in homes and businesses is disrupted. Fresh water has to be trucked in and given out because the water supply is usually contaminated. Food may have to be provided by relief agencies. Survivors may be without electricity, gas and oil. This means they will not be able to cook or have hot water or heat. Even if the electricity is turned back on, it may be days before anything is working. So repair crews are brought in from areas not affected by the flood to help people get their equipment back to working order. And the overall cleanup may take months.

Residents living in low areas along the coast, near rivers and streams and along flood plains and wetlands need to know basic safety rules. These include having sandbags handy, along with plywood and other lumber. People need to keep extra food, especially the kind that does not need cooking. Fresh water should be stored. A portable radio and flashlights with fresh batteries should be on hand. People with boats should keep them ready and supplied with first-aid equipment and food. Most important, everyone must know the way to higher ground . . . and if it is high enough.

However, people cannot control nature. Tropical rainstorms will continue to form. Hurricanes will blow in from the tropics. Thunderstorms will emerge from clashing weather systems, and there will be tons of water dropping from the skies. In the mountains snow will melt and someplace a dam will be strained or a levee or dike will break. The result will be floods.

If people have built their homes or businesses on flood plains, or on or near low-lying areas such as bogs, marshes, beaches or dunes, then they will be in danger of being wiped out by floods. In the past floods have caused millions of dollars' worth of damage. Many lives have been lost. No matter what people do to control floods, these natural disasters cannot be stopped. However, laws could be enacted that prevent people from living where there is flood danger. But it is not easy to stop people from living where they want to live. So it seems that future floods will continue to claim lives and property for a long time to come.

Some Famous Floods

1099   High tides and storm waves flood the coast of England, and 100,000 die.

1287   A seawall collapses in the Netherlands, and 50,000 die; a flood in China also kills some 50,000 people.

1421   In the Netherlands, a seawall breaks at the Zuider Zee Dike, flooding 72 villages.

1642   Rebels destroy river dikes in China at Kaifeng, flooding cities and lowlands; 300,000 die.

1824   In the Neva River in Russia, an ice jam floods Saint Petersburg, killing 10,000.

1864   The Humber River in England overflows when the Dale Dike breaks, with 240 dead.

1887   The Yellow River overflows in China, with 50,000 square miles of flooding and a loss of life estimated at 900,000.

1889   South Fork Dam in Johnstown, Pennsylvania, breaks, and 2,209 die.

1903   Heavy rains in Kansas City, Missouri, cause a flood, leaving 200 dead and 8,000 homeless.

1937   The U.S. Weather Bureau estimates that 156 trillion tons of water fall during the month of January, displacing 700,000 people.

1939   In North China, 500,000 people die in river flooding, and millions more perish in the famine that follows.

1948   Coastal flooding in Foochow, China, due to typhoon rains, kills 3,500.

Glossary

avalanche The sliding or falling of rocks, snow or other materials down the side of a mountain.

barrier beach A strip of sand running along a coast, which protects the mainland from waves and erosion.

coastal flooding Seashore flooding caused by high tides usually brought about by storms.

concrete dam A man-made dam erected across a river valley to hold back water.

dam A barrier made of any material, which stops the flow of rivers and streams.

dike A barrier usually made of earth, which runs alongside a river to keep it from overflowing at high water.

earthen dams Dams made up of earth and stone.

earthquake A trembling and shaking of the earth's surface.

erosion The natural wearing away or weathering of rocks or soil.

flash flood The flooding of an area that occurs in a matter of hours.

flood The covering or submerging by water of land that is usually dry.

floodgates Locks or gates built across a river, which can be opened or closed to prevent flooding downstream.

flood plain The plain next to a river where flooding occurs.

global warming The theory that average temperatures will rise throughout the world.

hurricane A severe tropical storm with winds over 75 miles an hour.

landslides The falling of masses of earth or rock.

levee A barrier usually made of earth or clay, which runs alongside a waterway to keep it from overflowing.

meteorologists Scientists who study and predict the weather.

National Oceanic and Atmospheric Administration (NOAA) A government agency that in part is concerned with weather and flooding.

reservoir A body of water stored in an artificial or natural pond or lake.

seismologists Scientists who study earthquakes.

storm surge A rise in sea level along the coast as a result of high storm winds.

theory An explanation of how facts fit together and a guess at what can be expected to happen.

thunderhead The top part of a thundercloud.

tropical storm An ocean storm that forms in the tropics.

tropics The very warm, humid region lying north and south of the equator. The sun's rays are strongest there.

tsunami A large ocean wave usually caused by an underwater earthquake or a volcanic explosion.

turbine A machine that uses fluids to turn a wheel or cylinder to create energy, usually electricity.

weather satellites Unmanned spaceships in orbit up to 22,000 miles above the earth. They have cameras that photograph the planet and send signals to receiving stations on earth.

wetlands Land, such as a bog or marsh, that has wet and spongy soil.

For Further Reading

Brown, Walter R., and Billye W. Cutchen. *Historical Catastrophes: Floods*. Addison Wesley, 1975.

Clark, Champ. *Flood*. Planet Earth Series. Alexandria, VA: Time-Life, 1982.

Cornell, James. *The Great International Disaster Book*. New York: Charles Scribner's Sons, 1976.

Garrison, Webb. *Disasters That Made History*. Nashville, TN: Abingdon Press, 1973.

Hoyt, William G., and Walter B. Langbein. *Floods*. Princeton, N.J.: Princeton University Press, 1955.

McCullough, David G. *The Johnstown Flood*. New York: Simon & Schuster, 1968.

Myles, Douglas. *The Great Waves: Tsunami*. New York: McGraw-Hill, 1985.

Nencini, Franco. *Florence: The Days of the Flood*. New York: Stein and Day, 1967.

O'Connor, Richard. *Johnstown: The Day the Dam Broke*. Philadelphia: J. B. Lippincott, 1957.

Sutton, Ann, and Myron Sutton. *Nature on the Rampage*. Philadelphia: J. B. Lippincott, 1962.

INDEX